The Little Drop of Water Who Learned to Give Himself Away

by Jerry D. Kaifetz, Ph.D.

Jerrykbooks.com

"The Little Drop of Water
Who Learned to Give Himself Away"©
Library of Congress Control Number 2009904743

Written and published in the United States of America.

Printed by:
FBC Publications & Printing
Ft. Pierce, FL 34982
www.fbcpublications.com

Table of Contents

CHAPTER ONE

This is a story about a little drop of water. This drop of water lived in a far away ocean. Very few people probably know this, but drops of water all have names. This little drop of water was named Willis. Willis was a drop of ocean water who loved to travel all over the world. Willis never had to worry about how to get from one place to another; he just sort of hitch-hiked on the ocean's gentle currents. Willis loved this kind of travel because he was always surrounded by his friends and family. He liked good company and enjoyed the feeling of being a part of things.

Willis was so happy when the currents brought him up on those large continental shelves or in the shallower waters that surrounded so many of the ocean's beautiful islands. It was here that he was able to observe the most beautiful colors in all the ocean. He loved flowing over the coral reefs. These lovely reefs were home to thousands and thousands of brightly colored fish, as well as sea ferns that gently swayed in the sunlit waters. Coral reefs were home to many of those curious creatures like his friend, the blowfish, and thousands of other forms of marine life. He called this the "prickly fish," because when it became frightened it would blow itself up with water; this made big needle-like spines stick out all over its body. This is how the Blowfish kept their enemies from eating them. Willis loved the Blowfish.

Willis also liked the Trumpet Fish. "They look so silly," Willis thought, "going around trying to look like a stick." This was a very strange way to keep those big fish from eating them up. "Who do they think they are fooling?" Willis thought, giggling as they passed by him.

Willis also loved the brightly colored Parrot Fish. Some of the flying fish had told him about rainbows in the other world and how lovely they were. Willis did not see how even the rainbow's colors could match the brilliant colors of the Parrot Fish.

No two days were alike for Willis when he got to live on a coral reef. It was so much more exciting than those long, long trips across the ocean on a current. Sometimes he would go for months and months and not even see the sky or the ocean's bottom. He was always amazed at how many drops of water there must be in the world —"Zillions and zillions," he thought. How fortunate and blessed he often felt that he was one of them, and that he had a name and friends and a family that loved him. Willis' Mom and Dad had always taught him that no matter how many drops of water there were in all the oceans of the world, his Creator knew him by name. Willis knew that every little drop of water was very important to the Creator. This gave Willis a wonderful, warm feeling inside, especially during those long journeys on the currents when he sometimes felt like nobody even knew he was there.

One day Willis was hitch-hiking on a current on one of his longest trips ever. He had come all the way down the west coast of the United States on the California Current. Then he had continued south and become part of the Peru Current. This current was off the coast of South America, and it was here that he began to change his course in a Westerly direction. He was hoping that somewhere out in the oceans there would be some reefs or islands around which he could play. He had been traveling for the longest time and he truly felt like he needed a rest. Poor Willis did not know that there was nothing ahead of him now for weeks and weeks except water — lots and lots and lots of water.

One day on this long journey, Willis felt himself getting warmer. He thought that this might mean that land was close, but sadly for poor Willis, this was not to be. He saw a great big mountain under him one day, and then he remembered what one of his cousins had told him once. This was part of the Pacific Antarctic Ridge. Now he knew why he felt so warm: he must be very close to the equator.

Soon the current began to take him south again. This was the South Equatorial Current, an older and wiser drop of water told him. Now he began to see the bottom. Yes, it was getting shallower! "Oh how exciting!" Willis thought.

He was so happy again as he began to see the beautiful fish he had learned to love and admire in the shallower waters. Willis passed right through the Marquesas Islands. He felt right at home here. He didn't seem to think that the long trip had been so bad now. Perhaps he would even get to spend some time here. "Maybe the current will just sort of swirl around the islands," Willis thought. He hoped that he could stay, but after a few days he noticed that all the other drops of water were moving on. How sad he was. "I wish that I could be like some of these fish and have a little house down in those rocks somewhere," he thought as he sadly waved goodbye to all his friends.

Now the currents took Willis south again. This had been good news when he was north of the equator, especially way up by Alaska. That meant that he would be getting warmer. Now, however, since he was south of the equator, that meant that he would be getting colder as he flowed south on this new current. Soon Willis began to feel very lonely. He felt as if he didn't have one single friend in the whole wide world. He passed by New Zealand and didn't even notice the beauty and brilliant colors around Chatham Island. This was not like Willis at all not to notice the colorful Parrot Fish or the lovely Sea Anemones. When Willis began to feel sorry for himself, he missed a lot of happiness that was all around him. Somehow he just didn't see any of it at all.

After a few days, Willis noticed that he was very, very

cold. He knew that he had never been this cold before, even when he had to spend that whole winter in the Arctic. Poor Willis! He didn't realize that he was feeling so cold because of how cold his attitude toward others had become; all this because he had been feeling sorry for himself since he left the Marquesas Islands. Willis was thinking so much about himself that he didn't even have any time to think about anyone else.

Now something began to happen to Willis that all drops of water in all the oceans of the world everywhere dread and fear. This is the one thing that scares water drops even when they so much as think about it: <u>Willis was sinking slowly but surely toward the bottom</u>! All this because of how cold he had become. He had seen this happen to other drops of water, but he never thought it would ever happen to him. Now it <u>was</u> happening to him and poor Willis didn't even realize it.

What a terrible thing! The colder he became, the faster he would sink; and the faster he headed toward the bottom, the less he realized how numb he was becoming. Once he settled on the bottom he would probably never be able to take a journey on a current again. He would never see his friends the Parrot Fish, the Blow Fish, or the Sea Turtles again. All Willis' friendly fish friends like warm water; they always avoid cold, dark water.

He knew he had brought all this on himself, and he felt so

badly. He became terrified at the thought of spending his life on a dark, cold ocean bottom. Then he began to see some of the most horrible, monstrous looking fish he had ever seen. They had great big green eyes and huge teeth. Their mouths were wide open as they swam by him. Willis was frozen with fear. He remembered now what his mom and dad had told him about keeping a sweet spirit and not feeling sorry for himself. He now remembered their warning about how fast a drop of water would sink when it became cold.

"Is it too late?" Willis wondered. He began to cry, now too cold even to shiver.

Just when it appeared hopeless to poor little Willis, he remembered what his Dad had told him when he was just a little water droplet. "Son, your Creator knows your every need; He will always help you if you ask him with a sincere and a pure heart."

Then Willis began to pray and ask his Creator for help: "Please, please, Creator! I'm so sorry I got cold and bitter. Please get me back up, and I'll try my very best to obey all your laws for the rest of my life.   Please save me! Please, please, please!"

But Willis just kept on sinking. He thought that this was the end. He felt like he was going to his final resting place: a cold, watery grave just below the Antarctic circle. How completely defeated and sad poor Willis felt when suddenly he heard a big "WHOOSH!"

"What was that?" he asked himself.

Hey, he was going up now! Wait a minute ! It seemed even darker than before. Yes, he was going up.

"What is happening to me?" he wondered.

He felt like he was in some kind of giant elevator. He could feel himself getting warmer, yet he was powerless to figure out what was happening to him. Then, the most beautiful, fantastic and thrilling thing that had ever happened to Willis took place. A giant "WHOOOOOSH" (even bigger than the one before) flung him way up in the air! Yes, the air! He had only been in the air one other time when a speeding boat splashed him way above the surface. Now, as he came back down toward the surface, he saw an old friend of his: it was one of the whales he had met when he was little. This old friend had scooped up the helpless little drop of water in his mouth on one of his deep dives and spewed him out on the surface.

"Oh, thank you, Mr. Whale! Thank you! Thank you! Thank you!" Willis shouted joyfully. Yet, in all the excitement, Willis never thought to thank the One who told the whale to help him, his Creator to Whom he had prayed for help in his darkest moment.

"Just following orders," answered Mr. Whale.

"I wonder what he meant by that?" pondered little Willis, the water drop, as he now floated on the surface that he thought he would never see again.

Now Willis was enjoying the peace and calm of the surface as he soaked in the warm rays of the sun. They felt so good as they glistened upon him, giving him that diamond-like sparkle that felt so new and wonderful to him. Then, in an instant, all that serenity vanished as a loud "BOOM!" shattered the afternoon air. He looked over his shoulder and saw a large boat. He recognized this to be a whaling boat.

"Oh no!" shouted little Willis. "Where is Mr. Whale?"

Then he saw his friend. The whale had been struck a deadly blow with the powerful cannon-like harpoon from the bow of the whaling boat. Willis began to shake and sob uncontrollably as they pulled the whale by him to load his giant, limp body into the big ship.

"I did this for you, Willis," the whale whispered with his last breath as the men pulled him alongside the boat, the ocean now stained red with the blood pouring from Mr. Whale's side. Soon the ship was gone.

Willis was left with a sad and empty feeling. He was glad

that he was saved from having to spend all his days on the bottom, but his heart was gripped with pain and sorrow at having lost his friend Mr. Whale.

"He died for me." Willis kept repeating Mr. Whale's last words over and over again. This was somehow more than a little drop of water could comprehend. He also remembered Mr. Whale saying that he had saved him because the Creator asked him to. "Just following orders," he remembered Mr. Whale saying. That must be what he meant. Willis was overcome with the thought of how much the whale must have loved him to give up his life for him. He thought of how much the whale must have loved the Creator to do what he did when he surely knew that a whaling boat was in the area.

The next day, little Willis saw a sight that sent cold shivers up his back.

"Oh my goodness, LOOK!" Willis shouted to all the other water drops around him. "LOOK! LOOK! LOOK!"

Willis pointed to the massive icebergs all around them. He had forgotten all about these poor, trapped, miserable drops of water who had been imprisoned for centuries in these great mountains of frozen doom.

"How awful," Willis thought aloud.

An older and much wiser drop of water overheard him. "Yes, that is the price they must forever pay for becoming cold and hard."

Willis' heart sank within him. Now he remembered. This is almost what had happened to him. He remembered sinking lower and lower, and how his bad attitude had started it all. Then he remembered his prayer to his Creator when he thought his end had come. He had thanked the whale, but he had forgotten to thank the One who sent the whale to save him. Willis bowed his head at that very moment, and as little tears rolled down his cheeks he said, "I'm sorry, Creator. You are the One who sent the whale to save me. There was no way that I could have saved myself. I am going to live for You now. My life and my heart are all yours from this day on."

Soon little Willis became part of the current called the West Wind Drift. He had made up his mind. He would never, ever feel sorry for himself again. His life would be different now. Willis knew that his life was no longer his own.

CHAPTER TWO

Several months had gone by since Willis had left the Antarctic waters. He had once again crossed the Pacific Antarctic Ridge, only this time much farther to the south than on his Westward journey. He spent long hours thinking about the changes in his life. There was so much in his life, his mind, and especially in Willis' heart that was different now. He was not the same little Willis on his trip back across the Pacific Ocean that he had been going West on the South Equatorial Current just a few months ago. The profound and deep realization of how much Mr. Whale must have loved him to give his life for him had left little Willis a completely changed drop of water. He regularly took time to think of what an eternity would have been like on that cold, cold, Antarctic Ocean floor. He even had some nightmares about those demon-like creatures he had seen way down deep, especially the ones with the big bug-eyes and great big teeth. What was perhaps most curious of all was that the blood that Mr. Whale had shed had somehow actually become a part of Willis.

Willis liked to tell anyone who would listen about how he had been saved by the whale. One day he met a water drop named Starky. He began telling Starky all about his experience, when suddenly Starky began to laugh and make fun of Willis.

Ha! Ha! Ha! Do you really believe that whale gave his

own life for you — a measly little drop of water? Listen, that whale was just on a deep dive and you happened to get sucked into his mouth on his way back up, that's all. You don't think a great big whale would let himself die just so you could get off the cold bottom, do you?"

All Starky's friends began to laugh at Willis. "HA! HA! HA! HA! HA! HA! HA! HA!"

Willis hated being laughed at. He knew that the whale had saved him. He knew that his blood had become a part of him. He couldn't understand why anyone wouldn't want to believe that. He thought he would try again to explain to Starky and his friends how it had all happened. He came upon them one day while they were all talking. Willis thought that if they could just get to know him and see how happy he was, that they would believe also. Surely they would believe if only they could see how sincere he was. "How wonderful that would be," Willis thought. "I'll just join in with them for a while; they'll see."

Starky was having a meeting with his friends when Willis drifted in. They didn't pay much attention to him because they were too busy talking. Willis didn't understand what they were discussing, but obviously something important was being planned.

"Hey, Willis," Starky called out. "Come on up here. We're talking about forming a wave when we get close to shore. We figure that if enough of us get together we'll be able to hit the beach with such force that we'll escape the ocean. Wouldn't that be great?"

"You mean, go up onto the Other World?" Willis asked.

"Yes, man; that's exactly right! No more drifting around on the currents, having boats plow over the top of you, feeling helpless and unimportant as just a tiny part of a big ocean. We're going to escape, Willis!"

"That would surely be something," Willis thought. He wasn't sure if he wanted to get involved in something like this, but he thought he would just hang around and listen for a while. Surely there could be no harm in that. Starky was a very good talker, and the more Willis listened to him, the more he thought of him as being a very ambitious fellow.

The plan that Starky shared with his friends sounded so exciting! As they came close to shore in a few days, they would break away from the current. Then the wind would carry them toward shore. As the water became shallower, the bottom would push all the water drops upward toward the surface. Then, as the water came up from below to join the surface drops, they would form a large swell and begin to accelerate toward the shore. The idea was to get up as much speed as they could in order to hit the beach as hard and as fast as possible. This is called a "wave," Starky's friends explained to Willis. A wave is the best chance a water drop has of escaping the ocean. Willis was intrigued by now, especially as he listened to Starky describe the wonders of the other world that would be theirs to explore and enjoy. He learned from Starky about other bodies of water in the other world. He knew when he learned about rivers that he would love to someday to be a part of one.

"Imagine," Willis thought, "just drifting right down through the middle of the other world and enjoying a scenery that changes every minute. Wow!" he thought. "What could possibly be any better than that?"

A few days went by. Willis did not tell anyone about the meeting he had been attending with Starky and his friends. He was told that his friends probably would not understand, so why bother to try to explain it to them. His friends, the current lovers, didn't know anything about real "freedom" anyway.

Now it was the evening before they were to come upon land. They were getting close to the big Island of Madagascar. They were now in part of the Madagascar current. They went over their wave plan one last time. Willis was excited, but he was also scared. He did not know anything about the other world. In fact, he was not so sure that the ocean world in which he had always lived all his life was such a bad place as Starky and his friends kept telling him.

"Oh well, that will surely change when they believe how I was saved from the bottom. Their whole life will change then," Willis reasoned. He had not yet had the chance to tell them about it again. He was waiting until they all became better friends. That way they would surely believe him; they wouldn't laugh at him then, either.

Now the morning came and Willis could see clearly the southwest coast of the big island. He could see green mountains, valleys, and all the beauty that Starky had described. Soon he would be a part of it all, he thought. How fantastic this would be.

The signal was given, and Starky's group began breaking away from the other drops in the current. Just as Starky had told them, the water began to get shallower. Now he felt the water drops coming up from the bottom and pushing him up. "Wow! This sure is quite a powerful force," Willis thought to himself.

He rose way up to the top of the swell that was forming. How exciting this was! Willis was right on top of the wave and he could feel the acceleration and power as he was being carried toward the shore in a great surge of speed and energy. "Man, this is great!" Willis shouted.

Then, just as fast as he had climbed up to the top of the wave, that same powerful flow plunged him straight down. Now he was on the bottom again. Willis was confused now and wondering what had happened to the lovely view of the island he had enjoyed just moments ago. No sooner did he begin to wonder what was happening when the surge back up to the surface began all over again. Now, here it was as it had been a few seconds ago — a beautiful view of the island, only even closer than before.

"I see," thought little Willis; "We are sort of rolling in together. I didn't know it would be like this. This is very confusing, and I don't like crashing onto the bottom like this with all those thousands of other drops on top of me pushing my face in the sand."

Now the pace was quickening more than ever. The water was getting much shallower, and the speed of the wave seemed incredibly fast to little Willis. He had always just poked along in a current. Now he was coming toward shore at a speed faster than he had ever imagined. He was being stretched out of shape by the acceleration and pressure. Everybody wanted to be on top of the wave, but nobody got to stay there very long. As soon as Willis got to the top, he barely had a moment to enjoy the view when "WHAM!" he was pushed out of the way by other drops and sent crashing to the bottom. Then he had to climb back up all over again.

By now the speed of the wave was positively frightening to Willis. When he came to the top he noticed that he was higher than the time before. The top was even starting to lean out over the rest of the wave as the shore came closer and closer. Now the shore was upon them, and Willis found himself right up on the very top. He was so scared! He would have given anything now to be back in the calm current with his friends.

As he had done when he was in trouble the last time, Willis cried out to his Creator. "Help me! Help me! Help me, Creator!" Poor little Willis was so afraid!

Just then the wave crashed onto the beach in an explosion of water, foam and sand. Willis was thrown with such a force as he had never before experienced. He just kept rolling and rolling and rolling until he was way, way up on the beach. He even reached some sand on the beach that was perfectly dry. Willis rolled over little ridges made in the sand by the wind. He felt absolutely dazed, bewildered, and scared out of his wits!

Now what remained of the wave began to recede back toward the ocean. He felt like he had gone as far as he could and would now be swept back to the water that he had been trying so hard to escape. Back down into a little gully he went. This time, he did not have the momentum to flow over the top of the little sand ridge he had so easily swished over on his way in with all the other drops of water. He just sort of rolled back into the little ridge that the wind had made and lay there without moving.

There were a few other drops of water still with him, including his friend Starky. "We made it! We made it! We made it!" shouted Starky, also exhausted and somewhat bewildered by the ordeal.

"We did?" answered Willis.

"Of course, we did, man! Look! We are in the other world now! We don't ever have to go back to the ocean! We're free! We're free! We're free!" Starky shouted.

Still, Willis was anything but happy. He felt so frightened and out of place. Now he would give anything to be back in the ocean!

Soon evening came and the sun set on the deserted beach where Willis and his friends had landed. Willis did not sleep at all that night. He prayed to his Creator and asked him over and over again to get him back in the water with his real friends. Starky and his friends celebrated all night long. Willis felt terribly lonely and out of place. He wished he had never met Starky. He wished that he had been content just to be a little drop of water — a small part of a big ocean, not a big part of a tiny puddle. Now he was stuck in a strange and frightening world without any way to get back.

The sun rose over the mountains early the next morning. Soon it became very warm. As the day grew on, the temperature climbed higher and higher. Soon Willis noticed a dreadful smell all around him. "Hey, what's that smell, you guys?"

I don't know," answered Bubby, one of Starky's friends, "but it ain't me."

"It is too you; you stink, man!" accused Starky.

Soon arguments and fights broke out, as the puddle became more and more hostile. It wasn't long before Willis noticed some green, slimy stuff on the surface. Now everyone was fighting to stay on the bottom of their little puddle. Soon that became distasteful as well, as bits of debris began to fall in all about them. Willis realized that there was no current in this little puddle they had formed, and, without the current, life was becoming most unpleasant for everyone.

"Oh my," Willis thought, "I'll never wish to be out of the current again; I feel so unclean when nothing is moving. Oh, how I wish I were back in the current!"

Soon more fights broke out as the afternoon sun climbed higher and higher in the summer sky. Now it was obvious to everyone that they had made a mistake in trusting Starky. Even his closest friends turned against him. By now, everyone's worst fears had been confirmed. They had fallen prey to one of the most dreaded and feared events that can befall a drop of water. <u>THEY HAD BECOME STAGNANT</u>!

Willis withdrew from the others as much as he could. "Maybe another wave will wash up past where we are and sweep us back to sea," he hoped.

All during the next night he prayed some more, crying and begging his Creator to help him get back to the ocean. He promised Him over and over again that if somehow he could just make it back to the sea, he would never again try to escape to the other world. Too exhausted from lack of sleep, he just mumbled into the night, over and over again, ". . . never again, never again, never . . . never . . .."

The next morning Willis heard a loud buzz overhead. He looked up from the bottom of the clouded puddle that had become his prison and noticed a little tiny bug. Sound travels easily underwater, so this little tiny bug sounded like something much bigger. The little bug dove down to the bottom of the puddle and bumped right into little Willis. Somehow Willis found himself perched right on that little bug's head as they both broke the surface together. The cool morning air felt refreshing to Willis, even if he was coated with that yucky green stuff on the surface.

"I wonder what kind of bug this is?" Willis asked himself, when suddenly a huge shadow swept over him and the whole area around the water hole. He looked up and saw

up close what he had only seen from a great distance before: it was a real, live human person from the other world!

Willis was more scared now than ever before. This real person got down on his hands and knees and looked him right in the eye. His name was Michael. He had brown hair and brown eyes and he wore glasses. There was a pretty little girl with him whose name was Elisa. Michael and Elisa were brother and sister. They were on vacation at the beach.

The poor little bug, himself also frightened just like Willis, began to buzz all over the surface of the tiny little puddle, while Willis just hung on for dear life. Michael and Elisa just looked curiously at the bug for a while. Elisa didn't like bugs very much, but Michael sure did. Michael then reached down with a little shovel he had been using to make sand castles and scooped up the little bug with Willis still right there clinging to the bug's back. Willis felt himself being lifted along with the little water bug.

In a moment Willis could hear the sound of the waves under him. He could even feel the salt spray around him. "Could it be?," he wondered. Could he be going back to the ocean? Did his Creator hear his prayer and send Michael?

Michael then squatted down very low, the way little boys

do, with the waves barely reaching up over his toes. Elisa watched her brother's every move. He gently lowered his toy shovel toward the water, and as a tiny little wave swept into it, Willis, the water drop, was reunited with the cool freshness of his ocean home.

"Oh, joy! JOY! JOY! JOY!", shouted Willis as he quickly joined the little wave that now welcomed him among its water drops. The wave then became part of the rip-tide that flows back out to sea, taking with it all the water drops that had crashed on the beach moments earlier. In a short time, Willis was back out in open water, the green slime now washed away by the other water drops. He felt alive and clean again! He was so happy, and thankful and free!

CHAPTER THREE

Willis was so glad to be a part of a current once again. He felt a true sense of belonging and of being a part. He loved the feeling of security that this gave him. He would never forget how troubled and hopeless he had felt when he had allowed himself to get in the wrong crowd. He felt sorry for Starky and all the others he left behind in that awful, filthy, stagnant puddle. (What Willis did not know was that moments after his escape, Elisa, Michael's little sister, dropped her ice cream right in the puddle on Starky and his friends!) Some escape that had turned out to be! Willis knew that he would never again be tempted to rebel against the way his Creator had made him. He was a little drop of water in a vast sea, roaming about the world on ocean currents with zillions of other drops just like him. From now on, that would suit him just fine. After his experience on Madagascar, he felt a peace and contentment about his place in the Creator's great plan for the world that he had never known before.

One day Willis overheard some water drops talking about how they would love to be in the area of an earthquake on the ocean's floor. This caused tidal waves, they said. In listening to bits and pieces of their conversation, Willis could tell that they too were planning an escape from the ocean. These drops had heard of the dismal failures of other drops trying to escape in a wave. They thought that if they could just be in the right place at the right time, they could become part of a mighty tidal wave and sail way up onto the other world. Willis knew that he did not want any part of this. He had learned that it would not do any good to try to talk these drops out of their foolish plan. Willis just quietly shook his head and drifted on past them.

The weather was lovely where Willis had been drifting. He was now just off the coast of Tanzania on the Eastern side of Africa. He looked out toward the other world and marveled at its beauty. Then he peered down at the lovely colors on the continental shelf, and once again Willis became thankful. Although the other world was beautiful and intriguing, he had learned to like his own world the best.

Willis had now become part of the Equatorial Counter Current. He was drifting just to the south of the equator where the water was very warm. He crossed over the Carlsberg Ridge and a few days later over the Mid-Indian Ridge. Of all the ocean currents that Willis had known, this was probably the warmest. Other currents only stayed along the equator for a brief time. This current paralleled the equator from one side of the Indian Ocean to the other. A drop of water could go all the way from Africa to Indonesia on this current. Willis liked the idea of getting warmer and warmer with each passing day. Once in a while his mind would wander back to that time when he was the coldest he had ever been. This made him even more thankful for the warmth he was now feeling.

One day the sun seemed brighter than usual to Willis. Willis felt so hot! There was no breeze, so even when he came up to the surface it was impossible to cool off. He could hear everyone around him complaining and wishing they were somewhere else. Willis did not want to stay around drops of water like these; he remembered what had happened to him when his spirit turned bad, and the dreadful predicament in which he had found himself. He was just glad to be a little drop of water, knowing that he had been carefully and especially made by his Creator and to know that he belonged in the ocean. He knew that he was important to his Creator, for without drops of water, there could be no oceans. The only substance of which oceans are made are little drops of water just like Willis. This made him feel very needed and uniquely special.

The journey eastward continued. Willis could not see the bottom, but he was informed that it was far, far below him. Soon he would come to a place where the bottom was almost two miles deep! This scared him to think about it, especially when he remembered those horrible looking fish with the big teeth and the bugged-out eyes that he knew lived down there. An older drop of water told him that on the other side of the Indonesian Islands was the deepest place in the whole world. This was called the Gallatea Deep. Here the water was over <u>six miles</u> deep! Little Willis did not even want to think about how ghastly it would be to wind up in that fearful place.

   As the days passed, the Equatorial Counter Current took Willis farther east. His body temperature had now risen to a very uncomfortable point. Willis would not complain, even though he had never been this warm before. He felt light-headed, and not at all his normal self. One afternoon, as the sun beat down upon him, he felt like he could not endure the fiery rays of the scorching sun a moment longer. Still, the blistering sun beat down upon him without mercy. The days were so long near the equator. If only he could sink below the surface for a few minutes, maybe he could cool himself off a little. Willis knew that he was way too warm to sink even a few inches below the surface. He was stuck there, and every minute he was getting hotter, and hotter, and hotter . . ..

   Willis looked up at the sky. It was a perfect shade of pure blue. He enjoyed looking at the sky, and especially the big, puffy white clouds that floated way up above the ocean. He wondered what the ocean would look like from up there. "Surely it must be a splendid sight," he thought.

   Later that day the sun went down below the western horizon. The coming of night provided very little relief from the heat for Willis. There was still no breeze, and Willis was afraid that if he got any hotter tomorrow, he might not make it through the day. He could not sleep that night. Even the companionship and solace of the stars could not comfort little Willis. He had always enjoyed the presence of the stars so much. He loved the surface at night, especially when he would be the one to catch a ray of light from one of the stars and it would light him all up inside, as he reflected it back into the sky in a perfect little twinkle. All water drops love doing this, but even this rare privilege enjoyed by water drops held no enjoyment for Willis that night in the Indian Ocean.

Toward morning, when he knew the sun would be up soon, he prayed to his Creator: "Dear Creator, you know how much I love you. You are The One who made me. You took a little bit of hydrogen and a little bit of oxygen, and shaped them in Your hands and gave me life. Then You gave me a purpose and a place to be and a reason to live. You have always taken care of me. You even sent Mr. Whale to die for me when I was to be lost forever. I love you for all those things. I hope You didn't do all that to let me die here. I need Your help now. I think I need Your help more than ever. I feel like I am going to die when that sun comes up. I can't stand being hot like this any more. Please help me, Creator. Please! Please! Please!" Then little Willis began to cry; it was not a loud kind of cry, but a sad, little, sobbing kind of whimper — the kind that little drops of water make when all hope is almost gone.

Soon the sun was up, and Willis knew that something miraculous would have to happen for him to be spared. He

was certain that he could not survive another day of the intense, equatorial heat. He had found comfort in talking with his Creator. He knew that He would help him; he didn't know how, but deep down inside, he knew. All Willis could do now was wait and hope and trust.

It was late morning; still there was no land to be seen anywhere. Willis' body temperature had climbed even higher. He was right on the surface now, and still his temperature was going higher. He felt like he was burning up. Looking up at the clouds, he noticed how blurry they appeared. He felt dizzy now. He wasn't even sure which way was up. "I think this is it," Willis whispered, thinking that he was about to die.

Everything around him felt strange. He had never known anything like this before. He was getting dizzier now; he could barely see. He was so hot that he knew there was no way out for him but to die.

He looked up into the sky, feeling certain that death was at hand. "If this is what you have appointed for me, Creator, then I am willing to die. I trust you. Goodbye ocean," he whispered faintly, his strength having now fled him. Still gazing skyward, Willis reached up with his last remaining bit of strength. "I am dying now, Creator. Please take my spirit into Your arms. I love you." Then, in an instant, he was gone.

CHAPTER FOUR

Little Willis felt himself going up. His eyes were closed; he now felt strangely different. He was afraid to open his eyes, but far too curious not to. He opened them as wide as he could, then he looked down.

"Hey! I'm not dead!," he thought to himself. "Oooooooooh...!" He could not believe what he saw. He was way up in the air above the ocean! "How can this be?" he asked himself. Then he noticed that he was still rising. The ocean kept getting farther and farther away. Soon the white caps on the waves were barely visible. "I must be miles and miles above the sea," Willis thought. Fear gripped his heart at the prospect of coming crashing down onto the surface again. Willis had seen a sea gull crash onto the water once. It was a terrifying thought that he did not care to consider.

Willis then made another astonishing discovery, perhaps even greater than having realized that he was miles above the ocean: "Oh, wow! I'm not made of water anymore!" Willis exclaimed aloud. "Look!" he shouted, gazing at his body. It was the same shape as before, but now it seemed to be made of something different. It somehow looked like it had water in it, but it seemed so different now.

As he looked more closely at himself, Willis was gripped

in astonishment and wonder at what he saw. He was now made up of millions of little, teeny, tiny drops of water, all held together somehow within his body. Each of these tiny droplets captured the rays of the sun and became like a diamond, casting about the most beautiful colors that Willis had ever seen. So fascinated was Willis at what he beheld that he did not even notice that he was going still higher and higher. He would probably not have noticed at all, were it not for the beautiful cloud that now came into his view; it was <u>right on the same level</u> on which he now found himself.

"Wow!" Willis exclaimed. "I'm up here with the clouds!" He could not get over the wondrous changes that had taken place in the last few moments.

Then, Willis felt a gentle wind come up behind him and begin to carry him right toward the cloud. Soon he was right up next to the cloud. He had never seen anything so lovely in all his life. Nothing in all the ocean could compare to the beauty of this cloud. In a moment, Willis was swept into the cloud by the gentle wind.

All of a sudden Willis was surrounded by a sea of smiling, beaming faces. "Hello, Willis!"

"Hi, Willis!"

"Welcome, Willis!"

Greetings were coming from every direction. Some faces he

recognized, while others he did not. All these friendly faces seemed to know him. Now he could hear music, as more friendly drops with glistening, sunlit bodies just like his greeted him everywhere he went. He spotted a very familiar face among these. It was Marty. Marty and Willis had been friends in the ocean. They had traveled together up the Kamchatka Current toward the Bearing Sea. He and Marty had become very close, but they were separated by a little island on their northward voyage. "Is that you, Marty?" Willis asked.

"It sure is, my long-lost little friend!" answered Marty.

"Marty, can you please tell me what has happened to me? The last thing I knew I was down there in the ocean thinking I was going to burn up. Then I prayed, and then . . . well . . . here I am. I don't understand."

Marty smiled as he and Willis drifted along in the cloud together. Marty talked for hours and hours while little Willis listened attentively to every word.

Marty told Willis that what had happened was the most miraculous thing that could ever happen to a drop of water. He had <u>evaporated</u>! Willis found this very difficult to understand. Marty told him that evaporation is something that happens to a very few and very special group of water drops. First you had to have realized that you were completely dependent on your Creator. "This was never possible, Marty went on to say," until you were redeemed from your bad ways of the past." Willis knew that he had been redeemed. He would always remember the time he was saved by Mr. Whale.

Then Marty told Willis that evaporation was sort of liked being completely changed from the inside out. "When a drop of water evaporates," Marty said, "it leaves everything in its world behind. All its molecules remain the same, but each one of them is completely transformed. This new drop of water then becomes lighter than the water and rises up above it. Usually, it meets other drops of water in the air and a cloud forms. These meetings are such a joyous occasion," Marty went on to say. "All the drops in the cloud are so glad to welcome one who, like them, has completely trusted their Creator not only to redeem them, but to transform them and separate them from the world below."

Willis looked down and could see land now. He was seeing the big island of Borneo. He could see the waves pounding hopelessly against the shoreline. They looked so small from Willis' new vantage point. How sad and hopeless those poor waves looked to Willis. He asked Marty why all drops of water don't evaporate and enjoy life in the clouds. Marty told him that they were all trying to escape from the ocean their <u>own</u> way. Most of them were not even redeemed, he went on to say with a touch of sadness in his voice. Many who were, he added, had yet to give themselves away to the Creator and trust Him completely.

Willis was puzzled by this. "But life is so much better here. Why don't they do all that and come up here and live?" he asked Marty.

"Well, nobody up here seems to be able to figure that out. Some people say it is because the oceans are polluted, and a drop of water cannot evaporate when it is clinging to its dirt; I don't know if this is the reason or not, but I believe that any of them could let go of the dirt inside them if they really wanted to. I am sure they would if they just knew how beautiful life was up here," Marty said. A tiny little tear had formed in the corner of his eye now, as he sadly looked down on all the drops of water in the distant ocean below.

Willis loved life in the cloud. He had never dreamed of anything like this before. Instead of looking up at the birds, he now looked down upon them. He did not even have to work hard flapping his wings like the birds; all he had to do was just drift along. He drifted all the way around the world his first month in the cloud. He had seen the mountains of Mexico, the colorful islands of the West Indies with their millions of delightful flowers, the Atlantic

Ocean, the continent of Africa, and the Indian Ocean. He had seen hundreds of boats, planes flying right by him, and so many other wondrous things. At times he thought that even Heaven could not be any better than this new life in the cloud. Could this place be Heaven, Willis wondered to himself?

Several times each week all the droplets would gather together. One of them would stand up and lead them in singing songs. Willis loved these songs, and he was fast learning all the words. Some of them were about how thankful they all were that they were redeemed. He could not sing these songs without his mind going back to that day in the Southwestern Pacific Basin when he sank to the bottom. How could Willis ever forget that day? Willis would even cry when he remembered that cold, cold water stained red with the blood of the whale. (Even now he could still see the traces of Mr. Whale's blood in side him; it had never left him and no day ever went by that Willis did not think about that great event in his life.)   Some songs were about the joy of being part of the cloud and how amazing and joyous it was to just drift around the world together. After the singing, one of the drops would speak to the rest of the cloud members. He would encourage them to be good to each other, to pray for each other, and always to be thankful to the Creator for allowing them to be in such a wonderful cloud. Little Willis always paid close attention to these messages. Often his heart would be touched, and he would bow his head at the end and ask the

Creator to help him be what he should.

One day another speaker came to the cloud. Someone told Willis that this speaker just went from cloud to cloud helping the cloud members. Willis thought it was probably because one speaker addressing the same group of droplets was bound to run out of things to say sooner or later. He was glad to hear someone new, and sat eager and poised, ready to listen to every word this new speaker had to say.

This speaker was a little different from the one Willis had become accustomed to hearing. He wasn't quite as polished as the other fellow, but he seemed very sincere and earnest in his effort to reach out to those who came. He didn't talk much about the beauty of the cloud, or cloud members being kind to each other, or any of the other things that Willis was used to hearing. He said that although all these things were good, that they were not the reason that drops of water were created, or redeemed, or evaporated. He said that there was a great need in the other world. He said that many countries were experiencing a something called a drought. He explained that a drought occurs when no rain has fallen from the clouds in a long, long time. Willis had never heard of rain. He didn't mean to, but he had a perplexed look on his face. The speaker looked at him with a look of understanding and kindness, realizing that Willis did not know the meaning of rain. Willis also noticed that some of the members had become upset when the speaker mentioned rain. They were whispering to each other, while others just fidgeted in their seats.

"Young fellow," the speaker called out to Willis, "I see that you do not know what rain is." Willis felt so embarrassed that he had attracted attention to himself in this manner. His face turned red as the speaker began to explain in such an understanding way the meaning of rain. Rain, he said, was the purpose of a water drop. He explained how that when the Creator made them, He intended for them to some day fall to the ground and give life to the earth. This could never happen while they were in the ocean. Only after they had been redeemed and evaporated could they come to the clouds. "Clouds are the only place from which rain can come," he said. Without rain, all life would cease.

At the end of the message, Willis bowed his head and told the Creator that if He had made him for rain, then that is what he wanted to be. Willis did not know very much about rain, but he felt in his heart that the speaker had spoken the truth in his message. No matter what, he would become a raindrop.

On his way out, Willis could see that some of the members were upset with the speaker. He overheard an older member say that this speaker would not be back to speak in their cloud. Willis told the speaker of his decision to become a raindrop. As he did, he could not help noticing the expression of joy and gratitude in the speaker's eyes.

Willis could tell that the speaker was old and probably did not have a lot of years left. He could also tell that he believed in rain and had been speaking about it for a long, long time. He had met a drop with a purpose, and he knew it. Now, he had a purpose too.

CHAPTER FIVE

Willis felt that he had come to a remarkable and fabulous point in his life. He knew that at last he had come upon the very meaning and purpose of his existence. He now knew the very reason that he had been made! What a feeling to know this at long last! Little Willis had a peace in his heart that he had never before known. He realized that even when he had felt happy in the past, he had never known real joy; what he thought was happiness had only been contentment. Life always seemed to be a mystery to him. There were so many things that he had never completely understood. There were so many questions deep in his mind that had never been answered. He had enjoyed meeting all the other droplets in the cloud, and they had been so good to know and to sing with in the meetings. Somehow, though, the one he had just heard speak was much different.

Willis did not know the answers to all the important questions of life. He could sense, though, that this droplet he had just heard knew many of the answers to questions that had remained unanswered in his own mind. That did not seem any wonder to Willis when he thought about the cold reaction of some of the older drops to his message about rain. Willis did not have all the mysteries of life revealed to him in that one message. He did know, however, that this fascinating new idea about a thing called rain was the key that would unlock new truths in his life. He had to find a way to become a raindrop.

In the days that followed, Willis went to everyone he thought might be able to tell him how to become a raindrop. He was surprised that many of the members of the cloud had never even heard of rain. Others had some vague idea about what it was. One droplet told him that rain was only for those who had been called to rain. He went on to say that, although rain was good and needed, he himself had been called to a ministry of comforting cloud members. Another drop told him that he could not become rain because he did not have "the gift," whatever that was. Some cloud members became very upset when Willis mentioned rain. They seemed to feel that rain was a very touchy subject. Apparently they had experienced an inner conflict of some sort in the past about rain. For days Willis went about the cloud trying to find someone to explain the truth of rain to him, but day after day his efforts went unrewarded.

One day he met an old and feeble droplet named Mr. Zebe. He found out that most other drops just referred to him as "Ol' Zebe." He had been in the cloud so long he himself didn't even know how long it had been. He was an old and wrinkled droplet, and nobody paid much attention to Mr. Zebe. Willis asked him about rain, and to his delight and surprise, Ol' Mr. Zebe did seem to know quite a bit about it.

Mr. Zebe and Willis would talk together for hours. Willis found out that there were some very definite requirements for becoming rain. Mr. Zebe told him that it was very difficult for a cloud to become a rain cloud without the presence of a few ice crystals. It seemed that it was unlikely to find ice crystals in their cloud, because some of the members would run them off whenever ice crystals tried to come into their cloud. Once a few ice crystal did manage to enter into a cloud, they would grow bigger and bigger; this happened because of the moisture in a cloud. Once they got to a certain size they would begin to fall; this caused these ice crystals to grow even more. The result was a snowflake or a hailstone.

Willis was positively fascinated at the idea of snowflakes. They sounded like a fairy tale to him, but something in him kept telling him that Ol' Mr. Zebe was telling the truth. Mr. Zebe told him that usually the snowflake would melt before leaving the cloud, or on it's way to the ground below. Willis soon realized after talking to Mr. Zebe for all those hours that his chances of becoming rain from the cloud in which he lived were not very good. Willis' cloud was a Cirrus cloud. About as close as a cirrus cloud could come to becoming rain was to leave trails of ice in the sky. Cirrus clouds are way too high ever to become rain. Willis learned that his best chances of becoming a raindrop were by becoming part of a Cumulus cloud. His chances would be even better in a Cumulo-nimbus cloud. In those clouds, everybody was for rain. These clouds were much thicker.

It was easier   for the up-and-down winds to operate, making it possible for the ice crystals to travel up and down in the cloud. These ice crystals gathered drops of water for the trip down to the other world as rain. That settled it for Willis! He had to move to another cloud.

CHAPTER SIX

Willis knew that he had to find a Cumulo-nimbus cloud. He had no idea what one of these clouds looked like. He did not even have any idea where to find one, or even how to become part of one if he ever did find one. He felt like accomplishing this task was next to impossible for him. He did not know how he was going to do it, but he knew that he had to leave his cloud. He realized that this meant leaving behind all the friends he had made. He had to become part of another cloud where it would be possible for him to do what he had promised his Creator he would do — become a raindrop.

Little Willis prayed every night for help in accomplishing this great task now before him. He had never heard of a droplet changing clouds, but it didn't matter if he was the first water droplet in the history of the skies to do it; he was going to change clouds!

One day, when little Willis was feeling defeated and discouraged, he looked way, way down below him and saw the most beautiful, white, puffy, billowing cloud he had ever seen. He was fascinated by this great cloud and asked one of his friends what kind it was. "Oh, that's one of those Cumulo-nimbus clouds," answered Henry, a new friend of Willis'.

"A CUMULO-NIMBUS!" shouted Willis, with an explosion of excitement in his voice that bewildered Henry.

"Yeah, a Cumulo-nimbus," confirmed Henry. "It's a pretty big cloud, but just about as crude as a cloud can be. They have absolutely no altitude, y'know. Poor fellows are so close to the ground; the view must be pathetic. Rather lacking in intellect and very shallow in their beliefs too," Henry added with a smug look on his face.

Willis hardly heard a word Henry had said, once he realized he was looking at a Cumulo-nimbus cloud. He just knew he had to get down there, and the sooner the better. All day long Willis gazed at that beautiful white cloud. He thought about it all that night, hardly sleeping a wink. When morning came, he was determined that this day would be his last day on his home cloud. The time had come for a change.

He had prayed the night before, begging the Creator to make a way for him to get down to the Cumulo-nimbus cloud. Willis' heart yearned to be a part of this great cloud. As the hours slowly passed, Willis began to realize that there was only one way for a droplet of water vapor to get from a cirrus cloud to a Cumulo-nimbus cloud: he had to jump!

The Cirrus cloud that Willis had called home since evaporating out of the Indian Ocean was at 20,000 feet.

That was almost <u>four miles high</u>! The Cumulo-nimbus cloud was at 8,OOO feet. That meant that little Willis would have to plunge <u>12,OOO feet straight down</u>! That was a free-fall of over two miles — enough to scare any water droplet alive half to death just thinking about it! What if he missed? Oh no! He mustn't even think about that possibility. If he was going to jump, he had to do it now — no goodbyes, no thinking it over, no second thoughts . . . He knew that anyone he spoke to about jumping to a Cumulo-cirrus cloud would try to talk him out of it, and Willis was sure in his heart that this was his Creator's will for his life. There was only one thing to do: he had to jump!

Willis walked way over to the edge of the cloud and looked down at the big, puffy cloud below. It looked so inviting as the afternoon sun drenched its giant tufts of white with the most magnificent brilliance one could imagine. Willis prayed for the Creator to guide him. He knew that this fall might cost him his very life. He also knew that his life held no meaning outside of surrendering to what he knew was his Creator's will for his life. He came even closer to the edge. This was it. He had to jump. With arms outspread, he gave a powerful thrust, leaping out as far as he could from the edge of the cloud. Willis had jumped!

Immediately little Willis began to plummet downward. The acceleration and wind were like nothing he had ever

experienced in his life. He was sure that he would never be able to survive this great plunge. Down, down, down he went, spinning wildly and becoming so confused and disoriented, that he felt like he had been thrown into the middle of a great tornado. The roar of the wind rushing past his ears was so deafening that Willis could not even hear his own screams as he continued to tumble end over end toward the great cloud below. It seemed like he was falling forever. He began to feel a strong sickness in his head and stomach that he thought might surely kill him, even if he did survive the fall. Willis felt doomed. He was sure that he had just made the greatest mistake of his life, and he knew that it would be his last.

Still, he dropped downward. Down, down, down, down he went. After what seemed like the longest few minutes a water droplet has ever known, Willis felt something very peculiar. He was slowing down! He was still falling, not having yet reached the cloud, but he was slowing down now. He felt a warm and gentle wind coming up from beneath him, and this wind was now breaking his fall. (Willis learned later that this kind of wind is called an "updraft," and that clouds such as the one he longed to make his new home often had many updrafts.) Slower and slower Willis fell, until the noise of the wind grew quieter and quieter. His end-over-end tumbling stopped, he began to regain his shape and ever so gently, little Willis settled down peacefully right on the very top of the most beautiful, glorious Cumulo-nimbus cloud that ever drifted over the earth. It was a miracle! Willis had made it 12,OOO feet through the air, and had landed safely in the billowy softness of a great Cumulo-nimbus cloud!

CHAPTER SEVEN

Willis was absolutely amazed at the overwhelming reception he received from the first moment he landed on the Cumulo-nimbus cloud. Although no one on this new cloud knew him, they were all so friendly toward him that one would think that they had all known each other all their lives. The droplets on this cloud knew that he had come from a higher and colder cloud and that what he had just done was a very courageous and remarkable thing. Willis felt like a very important droplet of water vapor. He could not have been any happier in his new home.

There was a meeting that night, and every droplet who lived on that cloud was there. Willis had never seen so many droplets in one place since his old life back in the ocean. This place was certainly different from the ocean, though. He could sense how much everyone there loved each other and how much they loved the Creator too.

The songs they sang that night were such a blessing to Willis' heart. Not only did these members sing about how joyous their cloud was and how miraculous it was to have evaporated, but they also sang a lot of songs about rain! Willis was so excited he could hardly contain himself. He wanted to rush right out the doors and become a raindrop right away.

At the end of the service, the speaker announced that there were some ice crystals coming to their cloud very soon. In keeping with the Creator's command to *"Go into all the world and become rain,"* he said that many volunteers were needed. He called on these brave souls to leave the comfort and security of the cloud to become part of a rainstorm. They would be coming upon the west coast of the United States, and there had been a great drought there, he explained. Apparently most of the clouds that had been blowing over the land were high cirrus clouds. None of them had been rain-type clouds, and the result was that the land had just about dried up. People down there were beginning to go hungry, farmers were going out of business, and everyone was praying for rain.

Willis felt a tug at his heart that he could not have resisted in a million years; he came forward as soon as the choir began to sing to surrender his life completely to the great need he had now realized. He had made up his mind: he would be part of the very next rainstorm. He couldn't wait!

CHAPTER EIGHT

Once again, Willis found his heart and mind alive with excitement and joy. He was so excited that he did not sleep a wink the whole night following his first meeting on the Cumulo-nimbus cloud. He felt as though he had grown up so much in the last few months. He remembered that just a year ago, the most important thing in his life had been those times when the currents would bring him upon a coral reef or a warm continental shelf. Those days of frolicking and hitch-hiking all over the world seemed so trivial to him now. He had no purpose back then. The only life he had known was the simple life of living to satisfy his desires. Now, all that had changed. Willis was amazed when he thought about how great a change had taken place in his life in such a short time. It was truly a miracle!

The warm rays of morning felt good to Willis. They were shining on the great cumulo-nimbus cloud from directly above. This was because the horizon was obscured by other clouds. Only the thin, wispy cirrus clouds allowed the sun's rays to shine down, and these illuminated only the very top of Willis' new cloud home.

Willis had prayed to his Creator much of the night, asking for faith and courage. Although Willis wanted so badly to become a raindrop, he had no idea what this new experience would be like, and he was very scared.

Soon Willis noticed a few particles of ice coming into the cloud from below. Before long, more and more of them began to appear. The dense population of water vapor droplets surrounded the ice crystals. They were so pretty to Willis. He had never seen anything as delicate and fascinating. A few moments passed as Willis just gazed at the ice crystals. Soon, he noticed one coming right toward him. He was so awed at its symmetry and beauty that he just stood there, silent and motionless. The ice crystal came right by him, and in an instant of time, Willis was drawn right to it by a quiet force he knew he could not resist.

Now, though a part of the ice crystal, Willis was faced with a dilemma that he had not anticipated. He was frozen! This was terrible. Was he right back where he was months ago, only up in sky instead of being at the bottom of the ocean? How long would he have to remain frozen? What if he had to stay like this forever? Doubts and fears flooded Willis' mind as the ice crystal drifted around in the cloud. Other droplets gave themselves to become a part of the growing crystal. Updrafts in the cloud brought the growing shape higher and higher. They were climbing faster and faster now. "Hey, I thought rain was supposed to fall down," Willis thought to himself. He knew he was going up, although it is very difficult for a frozen droplet to voice any real protest under circumstances such as these.

Now the ice crystal had grown to a large size. Willis was up toward the top of the cloud, and it was very cold up there. As a few more droplets attached themselves onto the large ice crystal, it began to slowly fall. It seemed that only as more droplets committed themselves did things begin to really happen in the cloud. Gathering still a few more droplets to add to its size and weight, the ice crystal began to gather speed as it dropped back down through the cloud. Willis felt completely isolated and helpless as part of this big crystal of ice. His only hope was his faith in his Creator. He had never let him down before, and Willis could only hope and trust that He would help him through this new crisis. Still, doubts flashed through Willis' mind as he tumbled back down through the cloud in this frozen ball of ice. "I wonder if I should have stayed on the cirrus cloud?" he asked himself.

After a few minutes of falling and being blown about, the ball of ice in which Willis had been captured dropped out of the bottom of the cloud. The temperature of the cloud had seemed to rise as they neared its lower portion. Now the warm air through which the ice crystal was falling seemed to be thawing its outer layer. In just a few seconds, Willis felt himself being warmed by this wind rushing past him, and before he even knew it, Willis was free from the ice crystal! He was now drifting down toward the earth. His body looked different to him. He was not a droplet of water vapor any longer. Willis had become a little drop of water again. <u>HE WAS NOW A RAINDROP</u>!

"HALLELUJAH!" little Willis shouted at the top of his

lungs as he fell through the air. He was surrounded by millions of other drops, all of whom had given themselves to the call of their Creator to be raindrops. What a bond of kinship and love Willis felt with these other drops. What a magnificent cause was theirs as they filled the skies! Willis was happier than he had ever been in all his life. He had never felt so free, so clean, so pure, or so close to his Creator. He shouted again, "Hallelujah!" He had never been so excited in his life! All of the other raindrops were shouting too as they fell together toward the earth below.

Looking down, Willis noticed that the ground was getting much closer now. This was the "other world" that he had heard about since he was little. In a moment, he would become part of that world — a gift given to it by its great Creator, and Willis himself was that gift. He was so overwhelmed by that thought that tears came to his eyes as his heart pounded within his breast. He was glad that the wind was wiping away his tears; he would not want other drops to see him crying. Just then Willis looked around him and noticed that other drops were crying too. "How amazing," he thought; "These drops all have hearts just like mine."

Willis could see some rolling hills below him now. The hills had vineyards on them. The vines looked dry and withered. My, how they needed rain! Soon Willis would himself be the answer to their need. He was nervous and frightened now, as he fell silently toward the countryside below.

Just as Willis came to a point about level with the tops of some distant trees, he prayed once again to his Creator for help and faith. This was all so new to a little drop of water who had lived all his life on gentle ocean currents. His Creator answered his prayer with a strong gust of wind that came rolling up the sloping hillside on which Willis was about to land. This mighty rush of wind helped to break Willis' fall. Thanks to this helping hand from his Creator, Willis was able to gently land on a little leaf in a row of grape vines on the side of a small hill. Willis' nervousness was eased at hearing the sighs of relief and the expressions of gratitude coming from the plants as they welcomed the falling drops. It was a beautiful moment. Willis would never forget it.

Willis gently rolled down the face of the leaf, now restored by the welcome moisture, and dropped down upon the dry ground just below. Followed by other raindrops, Willis and his friends were able to restore to the earth the water it had lost since the last rain so very long ago.

Soon Willis came across little, tiny, sensitive hair-like structures crisscrossing each other under ground. These were part of the root system of the grape vines. Willis was drawn right into one of these little roots and could sense that another journey was beginning for him. This one would not be as long as the one he had just made, but it was nevertheless a very important and fascinating journey. Willis felt himself being drawn up the root system of the vine, and before the day was over, he had found a brand new home. <u>Willis was now a part of a young, juicy, healthy Concord grape</u>!

CHAPTER NINE

Little Willis, the drop of water, was now entering a brand new part of his life. He was now a part of a plant. He was living in what had always been to him "the other world."

Willis had been drawn upward through the roots of the grapevine. It was quite dark, for he was now underground. There was, however, something warm and familiar about this new experience. Ever since he had evaporated from the ocean, Willis had lost his "saltiness." He was not terribly bothered by this, but now he began to notice that the saltiness seemed to be coming back. Willis had dissolved some salts in the soil, and now these salts were a part of him as he had climbed steadily upward within the roots of the vine. Even in the midst of this new and frightening experience, the salty taste made him feel secure.

Willis was fascinated with the structure of the grapevine, and in particular with its roots. All that Willis had ever known was travel and movement, as he had been on one long ocean journey after another. The contrasts between this life and the life of the grapevine fascinated Willis. He could see that one of the functions designed into the roots through which he had passed was to anchor the plant. "How wise it was for the Creator to have designed the vine so," Willis thought to himself. He realized that the older the vine would become, the stronger it would grow, and the more strength it would have against the wind and the storms. He began to feel that something had been lacking in his life as a roaming drop of water. Willis felt a sense of security and belonging in this new home that he had never before known. It was so good to feel this way.

A few days following his arrival, the sun came out. Willis enjoyed the feeling of warmth and security inside that young little grape. He had never known fellowship as sweet as the fellowship with the other little drops of water that had been arriving regularly since the rainstorm. They all had such wondrous and breathtaking stories to tell. Each of these little drops had wanted to find the true meaning of their lives, just like Willis. Being surrounded by so many other drops who had given themselves away was an experience beyond anything Willis had even been able to imagine. They would all talk for hours on end about how they had all tried in vain to escape from the ocean on their own. Many had suffered far more than Willis during those stubborn and foolish days. Perhaps these drops were even happier and more grateful in their new home in this other world.

Day after day, more drops of water arrived in the growing and happy grape. Willis noticed that the grape which he called home was actually part of a large cluster of grapes. He heard someone say that these grapes are called "Concord" grapes. It didn't matter much to Willis what anyone called his new home; he loved it, and he loved everyone in it.

As the summer months passed, Willis felt that his cluster was now weighing down the vine. On a windy day he could feel himself being swayed freely by the wind. The saltiness he had known months ago was now replaced by a beautiful sweetness that seemed to grow day by day. "Could my life ever be any better than this?" Willis asked himself. He surely did not see how it could. He had given himself completely to his Creator, and His Creator had used him to meet a very important need, and now he was part of the result. "How wonderful!" he thought. "How absolutely wonderful!"

One day in early fall, Willis noticed that the air was getting a bit cooler. He was well protected inside the firm, juicy grape that had been his home all summer. He did not feel ill at ease about the change in the weather, but he hoped that the warmth would soon return. Each day the period of afternoon sunshine seemed to diminish. The nights were so cold they reminded him of that awful experience in the Southern Hemisphere that had almost cost him his life. None of the other drops seemed to know quite what to make of this change in the weather.

Then one day, something happened. A young man with a big basket reached up and grabbed the whole cluster on which Willis lived and snapped it loose from the vine, dropping it in his basket. Soon Willis was covered by other clusters of grapes. Panic and fear gripped the heart and soul of every little drop of juice in every single grape. In a few moments, the baskets were loaded on a big wagon drawn by a tractor. Soon Willis' grape was torn from the others in the cluster, and each grape rolled down a chute into a giant, noisy machine.

How far removed this was from the peace and tranquility of the vineyard. How different this was from the calm, quiet warmth of those lazy summer afternoons on that sunny hillside. How different this place was from the beauty and serenity of the cloud. How different this was from the warm coral reefs where Willis had played in the oceans of the world.

Now Willis could see the fate that lay ahead of him. Soon his grape would be smashed by giant metal rollers, and his home would be no more. He could not help wondering if he had made a mistake. Should he have stayed in the first cloud? Was it a mistake to have become a raindrop and given himself away? Maybe he should never have even evaporated. Poor Willis quietly realized that his end was at hand. He could not stand up to that big, noisy, silver machine. It was his turn now, as he tumbled toward those terrible looking rollers. He could see the grapes ahead of him being squashed flat. Petrified with fear, he rolled into the first giant roller.

SMASH! Down came the big roller on the grapes. Willis now was forced out with a powerful surge; this reminded him of being part of that big wave one day when he sought to escape into the other world. Now he tumbled end over end down a steep chute. In an instant he fell through a fine filter. This made him feel as though he had been cut up in a million tiny pieces and put right back together again. Now he tumbled with hundreds of other drops into a glass bottle. In a moment he heard a loud "WHAM!" above him. A cap had been pressed onto the top of the bottle. In another instant a big steel arm swung right toward the bottle, seeming like it would smash it in a million pieces. "WHAAAP!" The big arm slapped a label on the outside of the bottle. It was backward to Willis, now trapped inside the bottle, but he tried to read it anyway. He just had to know what was happening to him and to all the other little drops of water. He twisted and turned, trying to read the label, as the bottle jingled and rolled on an assembly line with bottles lined up as far as he could see. Finally he began to see what the label said: <u>Pure CONCORD Grape Juice</u>.

In a few minutes time, the bottle was placed in a big box with other bottles just like it. A man pushed the box along some metal rollers and on to a great big, wooden pallet. Soon a fork lift lifted up all those cases of grape juice and rolled them right into a waiting truck. Another man closed the back doors of the big truck, and Willis zoomed off.

Poor little Willis was so frightened. He didn't know where he was going. He didn't know what his future might be. It was dark and cold in that glass bottle, as he bounced along inside that truck. Willis had been in other situations that had looked gloomy before. His Creator had always seen him through those times safely. He knew in his heart that he must continue to trust Him, even when everything seemed confused and hopeless. He began to pray: "I gave myself to You a long time ago," Willis whispered quietly to his Creator. "I belong to You, so I know You will take care of me. Please help all my little friends in here. They gave themselves to You too. Please comfort them. Help them to trust You."

Willis felt a very quiet and warm kind of peace settle over him. Somehow, he knew deep down in his heart that everything was going to be alright. He knew that his Creator was all-powerful, and that meant He could take perfect care of him. He knew that his Creator was all-wise, and that meant that He knew exactly what was best for him. He knew that his Creator loved him very much, and that meant that his Creator wanted to take perfect care of him in every situation. "Well, what is there to worry about, then?" Willis shouted out loud. All the other little drops of juice looked at him strangely, many through tear-filled eyes. "It's going to be all right," Willis told them. It's going to be all right."

CHAPTER TEN

Willis could not explain to anyone around him the feeling of peace and security that had settled in his heart. He had never felt closer to his Creator in all his life. It seemed that the more he trusted Him, the greater the feeling inside him that there was nothing over which to worry. Willis wondered if this was what he had heard others call "growing up." He though that this was probably not the same thing. He had seen many drops of water who had been around much longer than he; they were as far as could be from ever knowing their Creator, much less trusting Him. He thought, then, that this must be what others had called "maturity." He wasn't sure what this thing called maturity really was, but he knew that it was different from just growing up. Whatever it was, he knew it was something good. Perhaps this is what had settled upon him in the circumstances that were now trying him.

Willis knew one thing: whatever it was that had happened to him, it was making everyone else around him look up to him in a way that was completely new to him. It seemed that other drops would come to him quietly and just want to talk about "things." Oh, they tried not to let on that they were frightened. They always tried to make Willis think that they were just making conversation, but Willis knew that there was something different about these conversations; he could tell that they were very scared, even though they would not admit it. Willis could see that all they needed was someone to tell them that everything was going to be fine.

Whenever Willis tried to do this, he would always talk to them about how good it was to trust the Creator. Willis would simply tell them how he came to trust Him more and more. He would tell them all about the great love the Creator had for each of them, especially since they had all decided at some point in their lives to give themselves away. "How could the Great Creator not take care of us," Willis would ask them, "when what got us into the situation we are in was our trusting Him?"

One of the drops that came to Willis to thank him for his encouragement said something to Willis that made him think.

"Hey Willis, you know what?"

"What?" answered little Willis.

"You sound just like one of those speakers who goes around from cloud to cloud telling drops about the Creator."

Willis was stunned. He couldn't believe what he had just heard. He wanted to tell his little friend that he was not like those drops who spoke in the cloud meetings. They knew the Creator so much better than he did. They had a right to tell other people about giving themselves away as raindrops. Willis could not think of himself as worthy of comparison to one of those great drops. Nevertheless, he thought about how glorious it would be to spend the rest of his life telling people how great and loving the Creator was and to try to get them to see how much was missing in their lives by trying to do everything their own way, rather than trusting the Creator. "I'll bet most drops in the ocean haven't even heard about evaporation," Willis thought to himself.

Soon Willis sensed that the motion and bouncing that he had been experiencing had suddenly stopped. He heard some noise outside the truck that had been carrying him and his friends for what seemed like days on end. Although it had only been two days, it seemed much longer.

Willis felt some movement again. There was jostling now, and bumping and the noise of men talking. Someone was giving orders, it seemed. Willis thought that this was not a final destination for him and his many friends, but a kind of transfer point.

Soon the big carton that contained Willis was set down on the ground. The commotion had died down now, and Willis tried as best he could to enjoy the quiet of the moment. All of a sudden, he heard something that he could hardly believe. "SHHHH! Listen everybody!" Willis shouted to all his friends. "Listen!" Could it be what it

sounded like? Was this possible? A sense of joyous surprise swept through every heart there. It was water! They could hear the sound of little waves splashing up against the shore. Suddenly a seagull's shrill cry pierced the air. They were by the ocean! Now everyone knew that what Willis had been telling them all along was true. EVERYTHING <u>WAS</u> GOING TO BE ALL RIGHT! Cheers went up so loudly that the little bottles of grape juice began to fizz and shake. Then, in the midst of all the commotion, Willis felt like he was in an elevator. Willis was lifted high into the air. Soon, he realized that they had been loaded on a ship. He had seen many ships in his travels, and now he was actually on board one! The excitement was more than he could contain. He could see out of the bottle now, and all down the shelf, bottles just like his were lined up. Each one was fizzing just like his. These were the happiest little drops of juice in all the world!

Later that day, the ship set sail. Willis was especially lucky to be able to see out a porthole right next to his bottle. The ocean looked as beautiful as he had ever seen it. The sun was shining brightly as the ship set out on a calm, warm evening. He had feelings swelling up in his heart that he could neither contain nor describe. He had come so far since having been a part of that ocean. He recognized it to be the Gulf of Mexico. He had been there before, so long ago. He wondered if any of his fish friends were still there. He wondered if the reefs were as colorful as he remembered them. Before long, the sun sank into a glistening reflection of lovely orange and red colors. Willis quietly drifted off to sleep as the moonbeams softly glistened in the deep purple of the grape juice bottle. He was almost home again.

CHAPTER ELEVEN

Early the next morning Willis was the first little drop to awaken. It was one of those times when he woke up all at once. He was so anxious to begin living the next day that sleep could hold him captive no longer. Eagerly, he tried to position himself to be able to see out the porthole. Every cell in his body thrilled at the sight now before his eyes. Willis now gazed out over the calm, blue water as tiny waves caught the first shimmering light of dawn. Willis knew of the life beneath those waves that blossomed forth each day with the rising of the sun and of the great need below those waves.

Willis kept to himself much of that first day on the Gulf of Mexico. He recognized the Yucatan Channel, although everything looked quite different to him from this unusual angle. He looked at the billions and billions of drops of water stretching out before him as far as the eye could see. "Oh, how I wish I had the opportunity to talk to each one of them," Willis thought to himself. His heart yearned within him to tell them of the life and experiences in the worlds beyond the sea. He knew that every drop of water that had ever existed wanted to be free from the power of the sea. He also knew that few of them would ever know that freedom, because they wanted it for the wrong reasons. Willis remembered Starky and all the drops of water like him. If only he knew way back then what he knew now, maybe Starky's life and the lives of so many of his friends would not have been wasted. Willis had so much to tell them. He knew that he had what every drop of water in the ocean wanted. If only he could find a way to tell them. Willis began to feel a sadness in his heart. Not even the beauty of the sun rising over an ocean he loved could comfort him. Tears began to form in the corner of his eyes. Other drops all around him were joyous and happy, but Willis felt a sadness in his heart that he knew none of them could understand. He had to find a way to get the truth where it was needed. He had to find a way.

Willis heard someone mention that a few of the grape juice bottles had disappeared off the shelf that afternoon. Willis looked out and realized that there did seem to be fewer than before. He wondered what had happened to them. Somehow, though, nothing could get his thoughts off the great need that existed in the sea all around the ship. That big ship was plowing right through a great big ocean of need. He knew that each individual drop of water had a story to tell unique to itself. He thought how each one of them must hurt at times and how unimportant they must often feel. Willis became consumed with the greatest desire of his life — to tell drops of water all over the world about the only true way to escape the ocean and the secret of giving oneself away.

Suddenly a big hand reached out and grabbed Willis' grape juice bottle. With a loud "THUD!" the bottle was hurriedly plopped down on a round serving tray. Another

thud resounded next to the bottle as a glass landed on the tray. A whistling waiter was now taking the tray through a swinging door. Instantly, the rays of the mid-afternoon sun enveloped the juice bottle, and all that was around it. "SPOOOT!" The cap that had been smashed on the bottle a few days and many miles ago popped off, and Willis and all his companions were poured headlong into a clean, clear glass. Willis was taken completely by surprise, and with all his friends, tried to piece everything together in an effort to find out what had happened.

They could see a man and a woman sitting in chairs next to a white table on which the glass was placed. He was a kindly looking older man. This was the closest Willis had ever been to a real live human person since he had met Michael and Elisa on Madagascar. Other brushes with people had been either very brief or at a great distance. Willis' curiosity knew no bounds. He looked and listened eagerly as the man spoke to the woman with him.

He had a tenderness in his words. They had just retired, it seemed. The man spoke of having held meetings all his life. At first, Willis couldn't figure out what he meant. He listened more intently as the man shared his thoughts with the lady. He recounted how many miles he had traveled over the years. He spoke of meetings in places he called "churches." He went on to express how full and rich and satisfying his life had been. He talked of the people he had led to One he called "the Lord." Willis soon realized that this was the One drops of water called Creator. He began to feel a special bond to this man.

"Could we really have both been made by the same Creator?" Willis wondered. He reasoned that there could only be one Creator. With the harmony he had seen in the great interaction of life in the ocean, in the air, and on the land, Willis soon realized that it had to be so. How delightful that He has another name. "Lord . . . Lord . . . Lord." Willis kept saying it over and over. He felt a new sense of warmth as his closeness with the Creator grew.

The man picked up the glass from the table, folding his aged and weathered hand around it. Willis knew that those were the hands that had comforted thousands of souls, as he listened to this man recall the great days of his many meetings around the country. He learned that these were the hands that had pointed many to the Lord. Willis learned from listening to the man of the Lord's death on a cross many, many years ago. Willis listened to every word the man said. He spoke for hours on end. Willis learned that the only way for human beings to go to a place they called Heaven was for them to put all their faith in what their Lord had done on that cross. It was there that He had died for their sins.

Tears came to Willis' eyes, for the moment he thought of someone dying for another, his mind took him back to the cold depths of the Pacific Basin. All he could see was the blood-stained water that surrounded him as the lifeless whale was dragged up into the whaling boat. "How wonderfully strange that something as important to all humans would remind me of something so special in my own life," Willis thought to himself.

The old man set the glass of juice down on the railing. He continued to talk, but now Willis just gazed out at the sea around him. He had so much to tell the drops out there that he thought his heart would burst. "Hey, listen! Listen!" he shouted to them. "LISTEN TO ME . . . <u>PLEASE, PLEASE, PLEASE!</u>" All the other drops in the glass thought Willis was going crazy. He brought himself over to the edge of the glass, pounding against it and sobbing uncontrollably. Tears poured from his eyes now, as he prayed for his Creator to allow him to go back into the ocean. He knew that this was what he must do. "Please, Creator . . . help me give myself away again. I HAVE TO TELL THEM. I HAVE TO TELL THEM! **<u>I HAVE TO GO BACK AND TELL THEM!!!</u>**"

That instant, the glass slipped out of the hand that held it. Quickly the old man reached for it as it began to fall, somehow catching it just inches below the railing. Only one drop had spilled; it had landed on the man's hand. It was Willis. "Here, let me get you a napkin," his wife responded. As she reached over to wipe the drop of grape juice from his hand, it rolled down to the tip of the old gentleman's little finger . . . and fell all by itself down into the ocean below. Willis' prayer had been answered again!

Before long a great crowd of drops gathered around Willis. He was very different now, and that was something that nobody could help but notice. Soon the ship was just a dot on the horizon. The crowd of water drops around Willis was now a great gathering. If any of those drops of water had known little Willis before, they would never have recognized him now. When he spoke, they listened. What he said, they believed. There was a great power in his words.

All afternoon Willis poured his heart out to that great crowd. He told them of the great hopelessness of waves, and how he had once pounded the shores in a vain effort to escape. He told of the great dangers of becoming cold from dwelling on one's self too long, and of a Creator who loved them — each and every one of them. He told them of the only way there was to escape the ocean — evaporation. He told them of the wondrous worlds awaiting any drop of water who would just give himself away to the Creator and trust Him to guide his life. He spoke with a zeal and a passion he never knew he could have. He felt a power in him that seemed to grow and grow as he spoke. Sometimes he didn't even feel like it was him talking.

All that evening Willis talked. Millions of drops of water gathered. The very next day a great haze could be seen over the Gulf of Mexico. Water drops were evaporating everywhere. This great haze spread out into the Caribbean Sea, and soon into the Atlantic Ocean. Willis was so busy he hardly noticed what was taking place in the skies above the sea, but people everywhere could not help notice. Water drops were evaporating faster than anyone could remember. Rain clouds became more abundant than ever before — so many, in fact, that the Creator had to divert some over the oceans because there wasn't enough room over the continents. Soon, deserts began to bloom. People who had been unable to grow enough food suddenly lived in the midst of lush, green gardens full of fruits and fresh vegetables. Food became so plentiful that everyone had more than they had ever dreamed would be theirs. None of the world's children would ever be hungry again. The oceans became cleaner and cleaner from all the pure water that poured down from the thick, heavy Cumulus clouds. Before long, many of the returning raindrops began doing just what Willis was doing — telling others how to unlock the secrets of life by giving themselves away.

Willis lived to a very old age. He became known all over the earth as " *the little drop of water who learned to give himself away.* " The world became a better place because of Willis —better for drops of water, and better for people.

Little Willis was just a drop of water. He used to think that his life didn't matter much, . . . but then, *he learned to give himself away* . . .

Other Books by Jerry Kaifetz

World Class Truth
Bible Principles in Sports & Adventure

Heroes of the Valley
The Story of Joseph
The Story of Moses
The Story of Job

Clouds Without Rain
Spiritually Ineffective Churches & How to Fix Them

The Bench – A Heavenly Conversation

Racing Toward God
My Christian Testimony

Listen to the life story of
Dr. Jerry Kaifetz
on the
Unshackled Radio Program

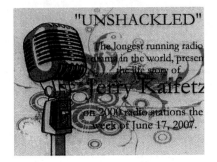

http://jerrykbooks.com
or ***http://unshackled.org***
archived episode #A2948

About the Author

 Jerry Kaifetz was born in Paris, France and educated in both French and American public schools. He graduated from a Christian college and seminary and then earned his Ph.D. in Philosophy in Religion in 1992.

Having come to Christ as an adult in 1983, Jerry's life in the world was rich, diverse and exciting in many ways. He skied competitively for fifteen years in addition to three years as professional throughout Europe and the U.S.. He is a certified Master SCUBA diver with many dives in the oceans of the world. He is also an experienced sailboat skipper and yacht racer and world-class adventurer.

He owns Omega Chemical (omegachemical.com), and has developed over twenty cleaning products for industry. He also continues to write Christian books as well as secular articles on moral issues.

You can visit his website at:
JERRYKBOOKS.COM